MY LITTLE ANIMAL FRIENDS OF THE FOREST

Romain Simon

TREASURE PRESS

French text for *The Baby Fawn* by Romain Simon
French text for *Flame the Fox* and *Johnny, The Wild Rabbit* by
Marcelle Vérité
English translation by Angela Wilkes

First published in Great Britain in 1986 by
Treasure Press
59 Grosvenor Street
London W1

Reprinted 1988

ISBN 1 85051 118 7

Printed in Czechoslovakia
50619/2

The Baby Fawn

Deep in the heart of the forest, one chilly spring morning
while everything is still wet with dew, a baby fawn is born
on a bed of grass and dry leaves. The sun and a robin
are the first to greet him.

The sun is just rising over the forest,
which looks pale green with the birch trees,
beeches and elms, and dark green where
the pine and fir trees grow.

10

The baby fawn is already trying to stand
on his long, shaky legs. He wobbles but
his mother encourages him,
bleats lovingly and gives him
her warm milk to drink.
The fawn snuggles up against her
and looks wide-eyed at
everything around him.

He makes a big effort and spreads his feet out
in the warm, damp grass. How good it feels!
He feels almost grown-up! His small shiny hoofs
manage to take grip in the soft brown earth.

A mole who lives there
comes to see what is going on.
She has a quick sniff
at the new-born fawn then
goes back to her underground home.
A blade of grass blowing
in the wind tickles the fawn's nose
and the scent of the wild mint
he has brushed against
makes him feel hungry.

14

The little fawn lies beneath the fronds of bracken
and patiently waits for his mother to come back.
Suddenly two lively little red creatures
with bushy tails appear in front of him.
'We are the squirrels, your neighbours and friends.
We eat pine nuts and hazelnuts. How about you?'

How wonderful spring is
for the baby deer!
He goes exploring
the forest.

A long-tailed magpie looks down
on him from the high branches of an oak tree.
The fawn delicately picks his way
to the spring to drink a little fresh water.
With his neck deep amongst the first tender shoots,
he stops to listen to the stags
calling and the sound of the does bleating.

17

A bluetit starts up
from beneath his nose.
The fawn scratches his face
on a prickly bramble and
looks in astonishment at it.
Still, he already knows
that a young bramble
is a very tasty thing to eat
and looks carefully for one
between the thorns.

18

Who are you, you soft
little grey thing?
The rabbit doesn't move.
He knows there is nothing
to fear from the baby deer.

19

20

The little fawn stops dead,
ready to run away,
when he comes to a clearing
amongst the dark fir trees.
An enormous mother boar
is taking her four babies
for a walk and they are grunting
and rooting round
in the moss.

21

Peck, peck, peck . . .
The woodpecker
is tapping his beak
against the trunk of the
old chestnut tree.
He is feasting on
all the insects hidden
under the bark.

22

What is this little grey creature?
A fieldmouse. And there is
a green tree frog
waiting for the evening
when he will join in a croaking concert
with the other frogs.

24

The little fawn carries on exploring.
He nibbles at tasty grass,
jumps over streams, and leaps
from rock to hollow, from copse to wood.
He lies down to rest for a minute and
stretches forward to take a look
at a green grasshopper in front of his nose,
then he disturbs a butterfly
who flits away in search of
scented honeysuckle or borage.

25

A grunting noise
down amongst the roots
in the dell, takes the
baby fawn by surprise.

It's the badger carefully
making his way down
to the river. The swallows
skim low across the water,
tweeting loudly. The kingfisher
is sitting very still.
He is on the look out
for little fish
for his children's supper.

28

The little deer goes closer
and flounders around in the mud
on the bank.
There is a piercing cry
as a pheasant starts up.
The deer has frightened it.
He has also
frightened the timid hare,
who quickly darts away.

29

The little fawn feels weak and tired. He needs to rest.
Stopping at a hole in an old tree,
he sees some hungry little hoopoes
waiting for their mother and father.
Their parents have no time to rest.
The sun shines down on the beautiful bird's feathers,
on the white flecks in the fawn's coat
and on the moss beneath his feet.

It is June; the little deer
is spending the night away
from his mother
for the first time.
He goes to sleep curled up
in a ball beneath a fir tree,

But the sun is slowly sinking
and it will soon be dark.
The little fawn feels
contented and drowsy.
Before he lies down to sleep
he goes to the beautiful pond
fringed by trees and takes
great gulps of the clear water.

32

worn out after his busy day.
It is a fine starlit June night.
While the little deer is sleeping
the animals who sleep
during the day
come to life . . .

Millions of stars sparkle
in the night sky.
The owl is flying
and hooting,
looking for insects.
The polecat is slinking
along the ground
in search of prey.

34

The fox cubs are waiting
for their parents
who have gone off
on a long trek
in search of food
for the family.

35

The little fawn wakes up.
He knows that he is
a long way from his home
in the copse, and a very
long way from his mother.
A weasel sniffs the air.
It feels heavy.
Drops of rain plop
to the ground.
There is a storm coming.

All the animals look for shelter from the downpour.
The little fawn runs as fast as he can,
until he is quite out of breath.
He keeps bleating for his mother,
who is looking for him too.

There she is!
The sky clears,
the rain stops and
everything smells wonderful.
A few raindrops
still clinging to the leaves
fall on to
the little fawn's nose
and he shakes himself dry.

It is already autumn.
The little fawn
spends his days
bounding through the trees.
But, if he hears
the sound of dogs barking,
he takes off in fright.

40

Following close at his mother's heels,
the little fawn sees winter coming.
He loves the quietness in the forest.
His feet sink into the snow and he seeks shelter among
the trees where he can huddle into a warm hollow.

The little fawn is growing up and will soon
have a fine pair of antlers.
He still runs everywhere, and he likes
the smell of the hawthorn, the tender shoots of
the birch tree and tasty mushrooms.
Before long he will be the most handsome
stag in the forest.

Flame,
the Fox

It is a clear moonlit night and the turtledove
has stopped calling and gone to sleep.
Flame, the fox, comes out of the bracken.
It is the foxes' hunting hour
but Flame isn't going hunting this evening.
Everything seems to be asleep in the great forest
on this fine April night.

Flame lifts his head and calls, then he waits.
Quietly, without rustling the leaves,
a vixen comes out of the trees,
followed by three cubs.
It's Rusty, Flame's mate. The family has left
its earth tonight and is going into the pine forest,
far away from men and dogs.

Their earth became too small for them,
but it was well hidden by the tall heather and broom.
They were very peaceful and happy there.
Rusty was able to guard her young ones as they
played in the entrance to their den.

The cubs are still very young
and a bit wobbly on their feet.
But they have a long way to go.
The new earth is high up, there on the mountainside.
And they have to get there tonight!

There isn't much time to rest before moving on again. Bandit, the strongest and toughest of the three cubs, is worried. He senses that there is something strange going on. All of a sudden the father picks up one of the cubs by the scruff of the neck and begins to run quickly. Rusty does the same with the second cub.

All Bandit can do
is try his best
to keep up.
Flame is very proud
of his brave son.

Bandit is worn out after the long journey.
But he soon starts to enjoy himself
in the forest again. The three cubs play among
the roots of an old fir tree.

52

He chases after butterflies,
mice and lizards
and watches the snails
crawling up plants.

They fight and tumble around
and end up in a heap,
one on top of the other,
at the entrance to the new earth.
The parents come and go.
Sometimes they bring back
a mouse and other times a hen,
which makes the farmer very angry.
The cubs are always trying
to have a drink
of Rusty's milk,
but she knocks them away
with her paw as if to say,
'It's time to go to sleep now!'
But Bandit isn't sleepy.

There are so many things to discover in
the long grass: hedgehogs that look like
prickly horsechestnuts, and freshwater pools
to cool your nose in.

Bandit can slink silently through the bracken.
You can tell he is the son
of a cunning fox called Flame.

Bandit's parents often worry that he has got lost,
but he always finds his way home again.
He likes to amble along,
then sit down in the grass
and watch the gnats dancing
around in the sunbeam.

One evening, as it is getting dark, Bandit is lying
in wait for dormice. Suddenly Orlando, the tawny owl,
who sleeps by day and hunts by night,
spots him and his eyes glint.
But Rusty comes running, clattering her teeth.
Orlando changes his mind and flaps silently away.

Rusty warns her cub to be careful, but he
doesn't take any notice. He'd like to go
down to the pond, where the big buttercups,
the forget-me-not and the rushes are,
but he is only allowed to play games
that will make him big and strong.

So the little cubs nip
each other, tumble on the ground
and jump up and down
on all fours.
Then they lie down
for a rest and watch
the green woodpecker
tapping his beak against the
old fir tree
in search of insects.

WOODPECKER

One morning one of the cubs gets a terrible fright.
She discovers a den and decides to have
a look inside. She doesn't hear the badger
rustling around in it. He was fast asleep

60

and is not pleased to be awakened.
The fox cub runs away,
scared out of her wits.

Now the cubs begin to
hunt like their parents.
They snap up snails,
catch mice and find out
that lizards who seem
to be asleep can
move very fast.
But Bandit hasn't forgotten
that he wants to go down
to the pond.
Flame doesn't take much
notice of his family any more.
He spends the warmest
time of the day
asleep under a bush,
then goes to cool his nose
in the cold water of a stream.
Rusty follows him and
makes him go back
to the earth,
by nipping his paws.

It is haymaking time on the mountainside.
Curious as usual, Bandit goes down to take
a closer look at the haystacks.
The farmer's dogs quickly chase him;
like a flash, the little fox streaks away.

The forest is full of the
scent of pine trees.
The crickets are chirping
and all the insects
are buzzing at once.
Madge the magpie
likes robbing the nests
of smaller birds.
Bandit would like
to do the same

and yaps at Madge
when she discovers
a nest full of baby birds.
The magpie
decides to teach
the cheeky cub
a lesson.
Ouch! What a sharp beak!
It's time to go!

In the evening all the cubs go back to the earth.
They listen to the blackbird singing as the first star rises.
They are a bit scared of the dark; they kiss
goodnight by licking each other's noses.

The summer rolls by
and the leaves start
to flutter to the ground.
Bandit rolls in them
but soon he will stop playing
because he will be
a magnificent fox
with a big bushy tail.

The fox cub likes watching his father fish.
By next year he will be able to turn
the stones over and flip shrimps

out on to the bank or
catch a trout dozing
near the water's edge.

The larches have turned
the same shade of red
as the foxes.
Everything in the forest
looks red and gold.

WEASEL

70

Many of the animals are stocking up their foodstores
for the winter. You can occasionally see a weasel
slinking through the grass. Bandit is
scared of weasels and runs away when he sees one.

At the end of September
some wild ducks
fly over the forest.
Flame and Rusty
keep a close
watch on them.
The ducks come down
to land on the pond.

72

Bandit wants to show
how clever he is.
He goes down to the pond,
gently puts a paw out
on to the green carpet
which he takes to be grass
and, falls headlong
into the water.

The ducks take off,
flapping their wings.
Bandit climbs out,
coughs, and tries to cling on
to the water lilies.
He falls into the water again.
Then Rusty grabs him
by the scruff of his neck.

How ashamed the cub feels
in front of his father!
He goes back
to the earth,
his tail between his legs,
while his parents head
for the woods in search
of fieldmice, dormice, jays
and the squirrels
who are busy
hoarding away their food.
Winter comes and the family
go their separate ways.
The cubs have become
fine foxes and can
look after themselves.
Their claws are
strong enough to
dig an earth, but crafty
Bandit manages to find
an old rabbit hole
where he can snuggle
up for the winter.

The snow falls and covers the sleeping forest in a white blanket. Bandit watches the snowflakes come swirling down.

76

A little robin pipes a sad tune in the chilly air.
Courage, my friends! Take great care.

The fox goes out for a walk round the woods.
Against the snowy ground he looks like a flame
flickering in the heart of the forest.

78

Johnny
the Wild Rabbit

Johnny, the wild rabbit,
is sitting on his hind-legs
and washing his face.
He licks his paws then
quickly wipes them over
each side of his face
and behind his ears,
just like a cat.

At daybreak, he left the warren, where his enormous family
lives, and headed for the clover field for his breakfast.
Wild rabbits don't like to stay in one place for long;
when they feel hungry they go where they can find
their favourite grasses, or just gnaw
at the old root here and there.

He is heading for the
wild thyme, which every
rabbit loves, and for the
fine leaves of the bindweed,
which he will nibble at.
Later, when he is
smelling of wild thyme
and bindweed, he takes
the time to wash himself.
Only the tips of his paws,
which are yellow from
the droppings in the warren,
stay the same colour.

Johnny has eaten his fill
of fresh clover now
and is making his way
through a field of corn.
He knows exactly where
he is going, greedy little fellow.

Suddenly Johnny pricks
up his ears. A dove is
cooing in an oak tree.
Do you know what
she is saying in
her own language?

'I come from the land where the birch trees
sway over the northern waters. Now it is Autumn
and I am flying to Spain.'
Johnny has already forgotten all about her and
is watching an old fisherman and his granddaughter
in their fishing boat. It is time to go home.

85

Hoppity-hop! Johnny is on his way home, slipping
through the long grass and under the bracken.
All he wants is to get back to his family.
The warren is very crowded. It is a
kind of underground town with endless corridors
and lots of exits; but he likes living with the others
and going to sleep alongside his brothers.
When they wake up they go out and scamper about,
but they are always ready to dart back to the warren
at the slightest sign of danger.

Johnny stops for a moment
to yawn. He's not tired;
he bounces around among
the wild flowers as if he
had springs hidden in his paws.
What's that?
A big cloud begins
to cover the sun.
It might be a good idea
to shelter in a clump
of broom and wait there

Johnny looks all round him,
his heart beating, but he
is so small, he can't see
anything at all.
What should he do?
Hide or thump on the ground
to warn his family?
But warn them of what?
He can't see anything!

until evening. But Johnny prefers to take a
little snack and nibbles a blade of grass.
Then he stretches, scratches his back
and smooths down his coat.
Who is that disturbing
the peace and quiet
of the morning
with those strange cries?

It's all right. Johnny
breathes a sigh of relief.
The strange sound is
Caramel, the hoopoe,
telling everyone that
it is about to rain.
And plop!
Three enormous raindrops
fall on the rabbit's nose.
He is very annoyed
and sneezes. He hates
getting his whiskers wet
and feeling the grass
sticking to him,
as if it was trying to trap him.

90

It's September and the sea
is crashing angrily against
the coast, but our little
friend doesn't know
anything about it.
How could he?
He is only four months old
and doesn't know about
the autumn storms.

Look! Caramel is flying away and there is
another hoopoe with her. No-one will
follow them and they are safe
in the warm pine forest despite
the shower, but they have caught sight
of the polecat, who is always hungry
for any kind of game.

Johnny is sure that this cruel enemy
must have passed his hiding place, so
he sits next to a dead branch and
watches the world go by.

It's not raining any more. What fun life is!
There's nothing better than frightening a frog
at the edge of a waterhole. Off you go, frog!
You know Johnny would never get into the water.

94

The little rabbit decides to take a nap on the moss.
The pinks smell so good after the shower!
He won't go home until the evening. No rabbit
who cares for his skin moves around in broad daylight.
In any case it's far more comfortable on this soft moss
than in the crowded rabbit warren.

'Caw-caw!' Who's that?
Johnny is always on guard,
even when he is asleep,
and he is off
in a flash. There is
always something going on
in the forest.
Nasty crows.
Why can't you keep quiet?

Feeling calmer, but still cautious, Johnny sits
down among the flowers to watch the dragonflies
zooming around after flies and gnats.
Johnny never hunts anything himself.

Thump, thump! Johnny
hears the drumming sound
of distant paws
beating the ground
to warn him of danger.
He quickly slips under
a blackberry bush and
crouches down very low.
And what does he see
all of a sudden?
A furry ball
hurtles into his bush,
flattens itself
beneath the branches
and keeps very still.
It's a very young rabbit
whom Johnny has never
seen before. She is
very pretty with her
soft brown fur, her shiny eyes
and her straight ears.

Little by little the stranger
moves closer to Johnny.
They sniff each other
and make friends. What do they
say to each other?
She tells him that she
was being chased by a polecat
or by a fox, both enemies
of all the rabbits.

But nothing happens. In any case it's not
the right time for the fox because
he likes to sleep during the day;
as for the polecat, he went away some time ago.
Johnny feels happier and nibbles at a cornflower.
Then suddenly everything changes and the girl rabbit
bounds away towards the edge of the wood.

She stops and turns her head towards Johnny, as if asking
him to follow her. 'What will he do?' wonders the squirrel
up in the pine tree. Johnny doesn't think twice.
His curiosity gets the better of him
and he sets off after the stranger.

102

There she is. She has stopped
in front of a clump of grass
which hides the entrance
to her rabbit hole. In
her secret nest
four tiny baby rabbits
are snuggling in the
warm sand, waiting for her.

103

It's a well chosen spot.
The fine, golden autumn sun
keeps the four babies warm during
the day and when evening comes,
the cosy nest, lined
with their mother's fluff,
keeps them snug and warm.

Johnny isn't interested in any of this.
He is too busy watching the lapwings fly by
on their way to the sandbanks, or peering at a
hedgehog foraging among the leaves. He waits patiently
for his friend to finish feeding the babies.

She's ready and they can go
and sample the first plump
and crunchy mushrooms.
Johnny is happy with
his new friend.
They will live together
and make a warren
for their future family.

But the mother will carry on going back to her
rabbit hole until the babies are strong enough
to look after themselves. Then Johnny and
his mate will run, jump and chase each other.
They are now the best of friends.
Crunch! crunch! go their sharp teeth
as they snap the dandelion stems.

They decide to make their warren at the foot
of a young pine tree. The soft sand flies
in all directions and the wind brings
the yellow autumn leaves tumbling down.

108

When the family is bigger
they will dig new rooms
and make more safety exits.
But in the winter,
when there is not much
in the way of food,
they would rather go off
to some vegetable garden
in search of
carrots or cabbage.

The baby rabbits from
the rabbit hole are
strong by now.
Watch out for
the farm dog who
chases anyone who steals
from the vegetable garden!

Life is hard for the poor rabbits in winter.
There is nothing but bark for them
to gnaw on and a few old roots and twigs
of heather for them to nibble.

The owl who lives in a hole
in a tree could tell you
all about it, but she is
very secretive and isn't
interested in rabbits.
In winter life is
hard for all the
animals in the forest
except for the squirrel,
who goes to sleep in his nest,
and the hedgehog,
who curls up under
some dead leaves.

The rabbits have to go out to stay alive.
They go through the trees and along the lakes,
eating a little willow bark or a few seeds that are
left over, then they quickly go back to
the warmth of the warren. Sometimes one of them
will cry out in his sleep. Perhaps he is dreaming
of pink clover, of juicy leaves or of
the thyme growing on the dunes
where the white seagulls fly...

Sometimes on a cold, moonlit winter's night
you might see Johnny and his friend
dancing in a clearing. They know that
Spring is not far away.

114